Henry's Big

Written by Malik Ducard
Illustrated by Richa Kinra

For the HDBros

ISBN: 978-0-9961488-0-1 (print)

For more Henry, please visit henrysbigwin.com.

Henry's eyes lit up when he saw the fun wheel in the arcade.

"Please, Dad? If I win, I will pay you back with more."

"If you win, a hug is all I want," his dad said.

His dad gave him a coin.
Henry carefully pushed it into the slot.
The fun wheel spun around and around.
And then it click-clicked out more prize
tickets than Henry had ever won.

The other people in the arcade clapped.
They shouted, "Wow!" "Woot!" and "OMG!"

The arcade owner ran out with a laugh.
He wore a funny cooking-pot hat.
And he gave Henry the biggest bear in the arcade.

But Henry pointed at the tickets that kept clicking out and said, "More."

The owner nodded and gave him the fastest toy car …
But Henry said, "More."

… And the biggest toy plane …
But Henry said, "More."

… And the coolest toy boat …
But Henry said, "More."

Soon Henry had all the prizes in the arcade!

But the tickets kept clicking out and Henry said, "More."

There was nothing else left.

The owner took off his cooking-pot hat, put it on Henry and made him the new owner of the arcade.

But Henry still wanted more.

"I want arcades everywhere!"
he yelled.

Henry opened more arcades.
He turned one into two.
Two into ten.
Ten into hundreds.

"I want arcades in outer space!" Henry said.

He opened so many that if you looked out your window,
one would look right back at you.

People called Henry "Kid Cool."
And they started wearing cooking-pot hats, too.

He had the fastest car,
the biggest plane,

and a boat with his name on the side.

Henry had a butler.
His butler had a butler.
Even his butler's butler had a butler!

They juggled hats and gave piggybacks.

They thumped and jumped and bumped,
until one day when Henry said, "No more!"

Because all Henry really wanted was to play with his dad.

So he said goodbye to the butler,
the butler's butler,
and the butler's butler's butler.

Then Henry walked back to the very first arcade, returned the funny cooking-pot hat,

and gave his dad
a big smile,
his last coin,
and the biggest,
giantest,
juiciest,
hug in the world,
because he knew
his dad would want no more.

About the Author

Originally from the Bronx, New York, Malik Ducard lives in Los Angeles with his wife and three sons – each a Henry in his own right. He is on the family and learning content team at YouTube where he gets to enjoy great storytelling on video, as well.

Henry's Big Win is almost a true story.

About the Illustrator

Richa Kinra, whose illustrations have appeared in numerous children's books, works with Blueberry Illustrations, a company of artists dedicated to bringing smiles to kids.

For more Henry, please visit henrysbigwin.com.

Made in the USA
San Bernardino, CA
06 May 2019